The Single Mother's SURVIVAL GUIDE

Patrice Karst

THE CROSSING PRESS
FREEDOM, CALIFORNIA

© 2000 by Patrice Karst
Cover design by Tara M. Phillips
Cover photograph © Vonda Hussey/The Image Bank
Interior design by Courtnay Perry
Author photograph © Tim Timmermans
Printed in the USA

For information on bulk purchases or group discounts for this and other Crossing Press titles, please contact our Special Sales Manager at 800/777-1048.

Visit our Web site: **www.crossingpress.com**

Library of Congress Cataloging-in-Publication Data

Karst, Patrice.
     The single mother's survival guide / by Patrice Karst.
        p. cm.
     ISBN 1-58091-063-7 (pbk.)
     1. Single mothers--Life skills guides. I. Title.
     HQ759.915 .K37   2000
     306.85'6--dc21   99-057494
                                                       CIP

To my sisters,

Single mothers the world over,
who despite their amazingly challenging situations, continue to strive
to raise happy, healthy children—
this book is in celebration and
praise of you.

Acknowledgments

I would like first and foremost to thank every being on this planet who believes in telling the absolute truth about what they feel, what their experience of this wild ride called life is, and who they are really. It is this type of person who keeps me sane in a "politically correct," often status quo, and rarely emotionally honest world.

Thanks to Caryle Hirshberg my editor for getting the vision and acting accordingly. To everyone at The Crossing Press who takes a paper manuscript and births it into being a real live book on the shelves for readers like you.

To every friend, loved one, or stranger who even once let me whine, cry, or laugh with them about this insane yet wildly brilliant journey of single motherhood (especially those who ever uttered those rare yet magical words, "is there anything I can do?")

To the inventors of kid TV dinners, cartoon videos, and fast food restaurants.

To my ex-husband who (though he royally pisses me off and will never have any idea what my dance has been!) gave me my greatest treasure of all time ... my child.

To each and every single mother out there.

There is a sacred and special place in God's heart for you.

To my most precious beloved reason for getting up each morning, laughter and tears from some place beyond this world, and who has taught me what I am made of and all that really matters in this world...my son Elijah.

To myself...for reasons only I can know.

And of course to God...the Creator of all, the Lover of all, and who has always and will always sustain me.

Warrior with love
Woman raising child alone
She is strong and proud

(The poet in me demanded "her" page.)

Contents

Part One

The
Basics

Who Is the Single Mother?

You come from every race, religion, age, creed, and walk of life, each with your own story to tell, your own rhythm to dance to.

You are divorced, unwed, or widowed. Some of you adopted kids, or had your children from donor insemination, or simply chose to have a child outside of marriage. Your partner may have left you while you were pregnant, you may be rich and have full-time help, or have four kids and struggle on welfare. You have teenage sons, or you may be a teenager yourself. You may have newborn twins, live on a farm, or in a skyscraper. Some of you have it easier than others, many of you are just about holding on.

You are everywhere, in all places. From the outside, you may look different from one another. However, all share a common bond— you are raising children without partners.

No matter how you got here, somehow you got here…My hope is that this book will have some personal message for all of you. We need each other.

The Fairy Tale

Once upon a time,
you went to a dance,
fell in love, got married,
had sex,
had some kids,
& lived happily ever after....

Well, maybe not happily. But the point is, until recent times this book would have had far fewer readers.

Well girls…
Welcome to the new millennium.

The Reality

We single moms are pioneers forging new roads. There is strength in numbers and our numbers are growing. In the United States alone, we are well over fourteen million strong and climbing fast.

We grew up believing that life was going to look very different from what we are facing now. Well, you know what? Believe it or not, we can make it even better than we imagined.

(Trust me here.)

Come let us journey together along this path of the single mother. Hard as it is—that's like calling Mt. Everest a hill!—it can also be the greatest adventure.

22 Reasons Why I Wrote This Book

1 To make you laugh.

2 To help you see that you're not alone.

3 To help me see that I'm not alone.

4 To try to make sense out of all the craziness.

5 To make a lot of money (honesty is a good thing).

6 To bring more attention to our plight.

7 Because it was needed.

8 To help us all get on with it, get over it, and get into it.

9 To help the children.

10 Because it's a subject I know well.

11 To give me something meaningful to do while drinking Frappacinos at Starbucks.

12 To make a difference.

13 To get on a talk show.

14 To make my son proud.

15 To make me proud.

16 To make the world proud.

17 To make you proud.

18 To get over my need to make everyone proud.

19 To give us all a place where we can unite.

20 To see my kid through college.

21 To make sure I'll get to go to heaven.

22 And...Because a little voice told me to.

My Own Story

My own experience as a single mother has been an unfolding journey that has taken me from depths of depression and terror I have never known to moments of such profound joy it was as if I had seen the face of God.

I have grumbled, cried, screamed, laughed, and alternately bellowed my anger to the universe, only to some time later profusely thank this same universe for the joyful experience I was having.

My story is not unlike many of yours. I left an unhappy marriage and forged into the unknown with a three-month-old baby in tow. We are in a process of discovering who we are, my boy and I, ever in motion, ever changing.

I wrote this book as my gift to all you out there who are on this journey with me.

May all of your children love you as my eight-year-old does:

I have a theory...

I think you'll like it. It goes like this:

One day when each of us are finished with this world, we meet our Maker at the gates to heaven.

Even though there are many people waiting, He calls for the single mothers to step forward. He tells us we are His chosen ones and He leads us to a magical land of jeweled cities and fragrant flower gardens where we are waited on hand and foot by angels who grant our every wish. He gives each of us a personally carved plaque and a trophy complimenting us and thanking us for accomplishing the stupendous job of raising children alone.

And then we are rewarded with an eternity in bliss, while those happy nuclear family wives with rocks on their ring fingers, personal trainers, and full-time nannies will lead a mediocre existence laying tile in our palaces.

I usually remind myself of this theory while scraping the crusted macaroni and cheese off of the living room carpet. I know it's all true, I tell myself. It's just a matter of time.

The Ten Commandments
for Single Mothers

I   **THOU SHALT** not be afraid to ask for help from anyone at any time (because the offers sure as hell won't come in by themselves).

II   **THOU SHALT** bring joy into your home no matter what, for joy is free and available to all.

III   **THOU SHALT** realize that this too shall pass and try to enjoy and make the most out of your life. Sooner than you think, these children will be grown, and, believe it or not, you will miss these years with them.

IV   **THOU SHALT** try not to speak ill of your ex in front of the kids, for, if you do so, it hurts their hearts and souls. If you need to get your anger out, talk to your friends or a therapist out of earshot of the little ones.

V   **THOU SHALT** love thy children with all your heart, even when they are occasionally monsters.

VI THOU SHALT develop a great sense of humor (if you don't already have one). It is surely the only way you will survive.

VII THOU SHALT believe with all your heart and mind that poverty and single motherhood do not have to go hand in hand and that dreams can still come true.

VIII THOU SHALT be gentle with yourself, take care of yourself, and remember you are doing a super-human job. This will help you to be a better mother.

IX THOU SHALT think of yourself as a hero, a star, an outstanding athlete in the sport/epic of single motherhood, and, no matter what, the show must go on!

X THOU SHALT try and remember always that you are not alone and that the rewards of raising a loving child is a gift given to you from God.

Reasons to Be Happy About Being a Single Mom

- It's happening.

- You'll be able to say, "I did it all by myself."

- Your children will be very appreciative of all your work. They will become rich and support you well in your old age.

- It will bring you *good karma*.

- Although you may not hear it often (or at all), you are respected and admired by many, including the Creator.

- You don't have to deal with a pain-in-the-butt husband in the house telling you what to do.

- It's pretty hip these days.

- It will make you a stronger person.

- Any kind of motherhood is a gift.

- Your other option is misery.

Famous Single Mothers

You.

    Me.

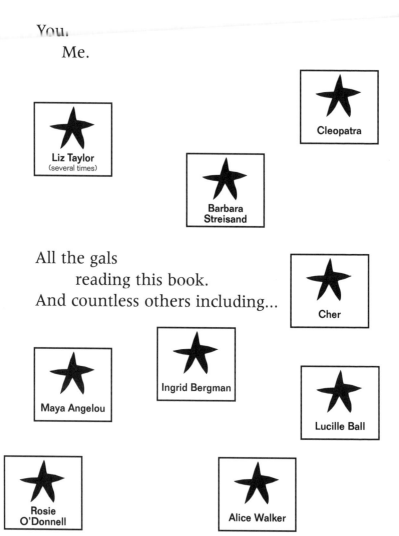

⭐ Cleopatra

⭐ Liz Taylor (several times)

⭐ Barbara Streisand

All the gals
    reading this book.
And countless others including...

⭐ Cher

⭐ Ingrid Bergman

⭐ Maya Angelou

⭐ Lucille Ball

⭐ Rosie O'Donnell

⭐ Alice Walker

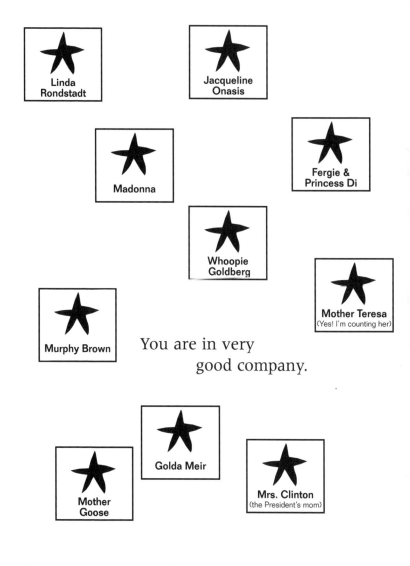

Linda Rondstadt

Jacqueline Onasis

Madonna

Fergie & Princess Di

Whoopie Goldberg

Mother Teresa
(Yes! I'm counting her)

Murphy Brown

You are in very good company.

Mother Goose

Golda Meir

Mrs. Clinton
(the President's mom)

Single Moms—
The Forgotten Segment of Society

We sometimes feel invisible and alone. Instead of being praised, valued, and respected, we seem to be put down far too often.

The truth is that we are courageous, strong, amazing women, doing, in many cases, a job raising our kids that is better than some two-parent families. The struggles we endure on a daily basis, spiritually, physically, emotionally, and financially, would weaken the fittest of folk—and still we carry on.

We have the same hopes and dreams for our children as everyone else and we will prosper and make our mark in history as the brave women we are, instead of filling the job of scapegoats for all of society's ills.

(God, I feel so political all of a sudden.)

When All Else Fails...

Have a good laugh...or a good cry.

chocolate

Call your best friend.

chocolate

Talk to God.

chocolate

Yell at God.

chocolate

Lie on the floor and pound it. Kick your legs and do a primal scream. (Tell the kids, "Mommy's doing an exercise.")

Rent a video, put on a robe, and make pop-corn.

Pull the sheets over your head and see if you can disappear.

Know that tomorrow will come
and it's gotta look better than this.

Ways to Nurture Y♡urself

- I promise not to tell you to take a hot bath but, actually, it's not such a bad idea...

- Read, re-read, use this book.

- Meditate. Lock your door, light a candle, get quiet. Even 5-10 minutes a day will help de-stress you.

- Be in nature whenever possible. You won't believe how different things will appear to you after some fresh air and scenery.

- Anything creative is great. Sing out loud in the shower. Dance in the living room. Get silly with the kids. Fingerpaint...

- Grow something: plants, flowers, herbs, vegetables. Anything will work. (The kid doesn't count. You need to grow something that doesn't talk back.)

- Find someone to trade massages with every week.

- A new haircut, book, outfit, or facial—something just for you at least twice a month. It doesn't have to be expensive, just some sort of treat.

- Feed yourself well; get enough sleep, and do some form of exercise at least three times a week. I don't care what it is: a walk, a run, skip rope—join a gym, ride a bike, get a video. Just do it. THIS IS AN ORDER!

- Keep a journal. Even if you just write for a few minutes, here and there, it will bring you a wonderful sense of comfort and a place to get closer to yourself.

- Always have something to look forward to: a vacation, an outing, a party. This helps keep you hopeful and happy.

- I give you permission to be selfish occasionally and put yourself first. It really is okay! (Martyrdom is passé anyway.)

- Repeat after me:
  "I am a goddess. I am a goddess. I am a goddess." (Let this be your mantra.)

Laugh often.
It's the best thing going.

Survival Strategies

- Let go of the need to be a perfect mother, immediately.

- Once a week, get a baby-sitter. Do a trade with another mom, whatever, and go out alone or on a date or with friends. (You need it. You deserve it. Do it!)

- Make lists. Pay bills on time. Return phone calls. Stay organized, then it won't all seem so overwhelming.

- Develop a support system. Make this a big priority. Make friends. You need others, and, yes, they need you too.

- Be easy with yourself and everything will be okay. Trust me, you'll get through it.

- Use the phone or go outside whenever you are feeling lonely and isolated. Reach out to people. You are not alone unless you choose to keep yourself that way.

- Stick the kids in front of cartoons or videos when you need to (no guilt). This will definitely help keep you sane.

- If, after trying therapy, depression or anxiety are really getting the best of you and nothing else seems to work, consider medication. Read my lips—"There is no shame in getting help to make you feel better." Do not for a moment believe you are weak if you decide you need this. It can really work wonders.

- Do not, however, overuse drugs or alcohol as your survival mechanisms. Believe me, it will only make things feel worse in the long run— much worse.

- Lastly, look for the light. No matter how dark the tunnel may often appear, the light is there. Find it.

  Oh, and watch for those mean, yucky, little gremlins that hang out in your mind some-times.

  Just tell'em to get lost.

Exhaustion

(I'll get to this page after my nap...)

- Go to sleep early.

- Take a nap.

- Eat really well. Pop vitamins.

- Breathe fresh air. Move your body.

- Take a nap.

- Ask for help.

- Pray for help.

- Pay for help.

- Don't take on anything else. You can't do it all. You're going to have to prioritize. The bottom line here—you and the kids first, everything else next.

- Learn time management.

- Did I mention taking a nap?

it takes.

- I hate to be the bearer of bad news but you may feel tired a lot. It will get easier the older the kids get.

- Rest when you can.

- Perhaps you can learn to enjoy it?

- Take a nap!

An Example of My Own Obsession

Just to show you how crazy we can all get, here's a little ditty from my own journal: Bear in mind that I'm average size, albeit a little softer and rounder than "the look." This should give you a laugh and prove my point. So, I admire my face in the mirror and tell myself that for a 40-year-old mom, I'm still pretty foxy—nice hair, face, boobs, but all hell breaks loose when I reach my waist. That's when every fashion magazine, movie star, hard body, L.A. babe nightmare begins to torture me.

I look like a balloon with legs and arms sticking out. I am a horrifying roly-poly, humpty dumpty, wiggly-jiggly freak. I am swine-like. I belong in a sty. A grotesquely huge belly; I'm a Buddha without the enlightenment. I look eight months pregnant. Someone should stick pins in me and watch me deflate flying around the room. I don't deserve to live. I must never eat again. No man in his right mind unless he was blind and had no feeling in his hands could stand to look or touch this body.

This is usually about the time I make a big plate of fettucini, call one of my best girlfriends and ask her to remind me of all my redeeming qualities, that I simply have bought into a pathetic media and societal image that all women should look like stick figures with giant breasts and that most men in three-quarters of the world would find me overwhelmingly sensuous, soft, sexy, and suckable.

I am a confused person.

Girlfriends, isn't it time we stop making ourselves crazy with all this? What do you think?

Different Ways to Say No

When you get asked to do stuff that you really don't want to do, simply say...

- Sorry. That won't work for me. Have you tried _____?

- You know I'm a single mother with too much on my plate already.

- Gee, no. I just won't be able to. Try me next year, next life, whatever.

- Are you out of your _____ mind!?

- Come again?

- No, but thanks for asking.

- No, but can I borrow some money?

- Hmm, I doubt it, but, if that changes, I'll call you.

- God, I'd really love to but my inner guidance says not to.

Quick Dinner Ideas

McDonald's

tater tots

kid TV dinners

Taco Bell

fish sticks

Mac & Cheese

pizza

Kentucky Fried Chicken

Have I made my point!?

Trust me, they'll live. And, no one ever ended up on an analyst's couch because their mom gave them a few Big Macs too many. If you have a lot of guilt around this, get over it! Remember this is a survival guide!

Body Image

I have one thing to say to everyone who thinks we should all look like Barbie. Remember, people, Barbie is a plastic doll with fake hair!

What can I say? We live in a sick society that worships bodies more than spirits. Be kind to yourself. Your body deserves love and care and gratitude for keeping you alive and healthy and able to see skies and stars and oceans, to breathe, dance, laugh, and sing, to touch your children's faces. This is what's important—not what size you wear or what the almighty scale tells you.

Look, I'm not saying pigout, get fat, and to hell with the world. I am saying: Ease up!

Love yourself; feed yourself when you're hungry; stop when you're full; love life; let everyone else obsess about food and bodies; you have many more important and joyful things to concentrate on.

listening?

listening

Dating Rules
or "The No Soul Mate Yet Blues"

- If he doesn't love your kids—don't love him.

- Don't bring a string of men through your house. It will confuse the kids and the last thing they need is more loss in their lives.

- You may not like this one, but here goes anyway. Your kids come first, period. It's a fine balancing act, I know. And, of course, you have your own needs, but, when push comes to shove, your kids will always be yours. He, on the other hand, may not.

- It can be so hard to meet men when you're busy being a mom. You'll have to try a little harder. Get out of the sweats. Put some makeup on. Smile and talk to five new men a week. Consider this a homework assignment.

- You won't find him at home. Translation: get out of the house every once in a while.

Hire an inexpensive sitter or find another mom to trade with.

- But don't go out all the time. I repeat, your kids need you.

- Realistically, you're not going to find perfection. But, I say, aim for pretty damn close. You're worth it.

- I know it's hard to even imagine how to fit a man into your already overworked, frantic schedule, so I suggest this one rule: if he will add to your life and help make things easier, he's a keeper. Conversely, if he will create more work in your life—bye-bye!

- Believe that you can and will find someone wonderful. It just may take more time than you would like. Keep the faith.

- About the whole sex thing—be careful and safe, not just with your body. Don't kid yourself. As women, if we make love, we bond. Good rule of thumb: unless you're masochistic, protect your heart. Be honest with yourself. Can you really have casual sex? Most of us usually can't. And, you know, you shouldn't underestimate masturbating. It's not half bad.

- The absolute deal breakers are: mean guys, cheap guys, dull guys, womanizers, con men, commitment-phobes, control freaks, misogynists, SNAGs (Shallow New Age Guys), guys who aren't great to your kids, guys who live in their vans, abusers, premature ejaculators, guys who lie, guys who don't do what they say they'll do, slime, compulsive gamblers, stupid guys, workaholics, weirdos, smelly slobs, guys who can't get over their last love, drunks, mama's boys, druggies, GUs (Geographic Undesirables), polygamists, guys serving time, married men, gay men, teenagers (unless you are one), or guys who need their green card. Also, "potential" is a word that I have a real problem with. What you see now is usually what you get!

I give you this list as a reminder because it may have been a while since you had any. I don't want your hormones to fog your better judgment. Unfortunately, I've now wiped out 95 percent of your available pool of men to pick from. Oh, well, la di da—I never promised you a rose garden, just the truth as I know it. There's still 5 percent good stuff out there. Go get 'em!

Single Dads

At this point, some of you may be wondering why I did not do the politically correct thing and include single fathers in this book. Quite simply, I just didn't feel like it. I am a woman. I'm sure many of these issues are the same for single fathers, too. But, this book is for us gals. I'm not sexist and I know there are many wonderful men out there doing a great job raising kids alone, but there are many more women.

If, however, you are a single dad reading this, you're welcome to journey with us. In fact, perhaps one of you will even get inspired and write a book for your brothers. (By the way, ladies, single dads are good possibilities for becoming terrific friends and/or boyfriends. You'll have a lot in common.)

And since we're on the subject, if any of you single dads are cute and available, pop me a line. (You've got to be resourceful, girls.)

A Spiritual Message:
Reach to a Higher Power

Whatever your particular religious or spiritual beliefs, please know this: there is a Power greater than you, watching over, and protecting you. Get to know it.

I know you may not always feel its grace. One of the most painful aspects of mothering solo is the isolation and the feelings of aloneness, but this Power is there.

Oh, yes, it's there. Call it whatever you want. Just call it. When you look up at the stars at night, see it. And, when you cuddle up with those precious children of yours, feel it. And, when day in and day out there is still some laughter and joy, know it. When at your most lost and lonely, ask it to guide you. To sustain you.

You have it in you to make it. It's all part of the plan. You were chosen for this role. Blessings abound if you take the time to look for them.

You are loved. You are not alone.

Building Community:
Extending Your Family

(Girlfriend, you ain't no island!)

Our tribes are gone. We need to recreate them. We have to get out of our isolation. It will take some effort, but, by God, it is so worth it. Some ideas to get you started:

- Really get to know your neighbors beyond just nodding hello once in a while.

- Look for a single mother support group or start your own.

- Ask everyone you know if they know any single moms they can connect you with. When you find them they'll be a source of useful information.

- Put an ad in your local paper inviting other single moms to call you. (Please give a voice mail number or a PO box for safety reasons.)

- Join organizations, clubs, groups, churches, temples, classes, co-ops. They are everywhere.

- Look into the Big Brothers organization for the kids.

- If you are lucky enough to have supportive relatives nearby, by all means utilize them and be grateful (many of us don't).

- You may have to reach out first, but when you do, many hands will reach back to you, perhaps not immediately but eventually.

- Anywhere you can get it, get it. Invite people to dinner, to coffee, for a walk, a talk. Friendships will nurture you as nothing else can. Invitations out equal invitations back. Be patient and persistent.

- Arrange play dates for your kids and befriend their parents.

  Remember this: People need you just as much as you need them. It's time we all start sharing more. It will affect our ultimate survival.

- Be on the lookout. Love is truly all around. Find it.

Discipline

It's harder when there's just one of you.
Bottom line—do what it takes as long as
you're not causing long-term psychological
damage.

- Praise and reward good behavior.

- Bribe.

- Threaten.

- Beg.

- Make sure to take your own "time-outs."

- Call the father (if there is one).

- Try tough love.

- Choose your battles.

- Consider boarding school (just kidding).

No Room for Misery Makers

It's okay to have friendships where you spend time commiserating with one another. In fact, it's downright necessary and can be a lot of fun. It is not, however, conducive to your growth or happiness to hang out complaining all the time. Nor is it healthy to have totally negative people around sucking your juice. Please pay attention on this one.

It is vital to create good company in our lives. Be around people who:

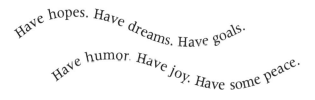

Have hopes. Have dreams. Have goals.
Have humor. Have joy. Have some peace.

I'm not saying you have to associate only with Pollyanna types, but if you find yourself with people not willing or interested in moving out of their depths of whining, complaining, misery, and it's bringing you down, kindly dump them and move on. Your own well-being depends on this!

What Matters Is Love

No matter what you read or hear about the ill effects of children raised by single mothers, don't buy into it for a second. It is simply unfounded, prejudiced, fundamentalist rhetoric, where the object is to guilt trip you. Sure, optimally and in a perfect world, we would have all liked to raise our kids with a wonderful, loving, available father. And sure, as a result of being single moms, we may not always have as much time, money, or three perfectly balanced hot meals every day as we would have liked.

But, you know what? What matters is love. As long as our children are safe, fed, warm, joyful, and grow up knowing we love them unconditionally, they will be luckier, healthier, and happier than most. Don't be a perfectionist.

what matters

Never let your ideals ever undermine your
knowing that your children are doing great.
Love them. Love them. Love them.
Everything else will fall into place.

is LOVE

Patrice's Reality Checks

I tend to get a little bitchy here. Please forgive me.

- Don't drive yourself nuts if your kids don't have the most expensive designer sneakers, etc. They'll still turn out to be fine human beings. Stop trying to keep up with the Jones's. They're boring people anyway, with no inner life.

- The next time some idiotic, married bimbo says, "I don't know how you do it. I never could," pat her on the shoulder and tell her that you feel sorry for her, because there's a 50 percent chance she'll have to. Smile sweetly and walk away.

- Remember this, too. When you see all those intact little families and you start imagining the perfect life they're all living—fairs, family vacations, and barbecues—picture this: every night, half of those women are lying next to men they can't stand because they don't have the courage to be out on their own, the way you did.

The theory that it's better to stay together "for the children," even if the marriage sucks, is hogwash. How healthy can it possibly be for a child to grow up in a home with parents constantly fighting or, worse yet, quietly loathing each other? You did a good thing.

The next person who says to you, "Well, when you learn to be perfectly content and happy with yourself and aren't looking for a relationship—then you'll find one," slap them for me, will ya? Better yet, call me. I'll do it for you. My pleasure. Of all the cliché, arrogant party-line crap...spare me.

Money $ Issues

I wish I had some brilliant, miraculous answers
I don't. Just some thoughts on what has worked
well for me.

$ I think it's a much better mindset to ask
yourself how you can create more money
coming into your life rather than asking
yourself, "How can I scrimp and save just
enough to get by?" Having said that, I
won't offer you any budgets or lectures on
how to become prosperous.

$ Just one tip, though. Ask for the "single
mother discount" wherever you go. If you
can get over any embarrassment about this,
it's unbelievable how well it works. Not
always, but at least 25 percent of the time,
I've gotten breaks on child care, classes,
products, services, movies—you name it—
it's fun and, darn it, we deserve it!

$ If you're entitled to child support, make
sure you get it. However, peace of mind is
priceless—sometimes it's worth getting a
little bit less and not battling night and day
with your ex. (Please see "Dealing with the
Ex.")

Consider sharing a house with other single parents. There are many benefits to this beyond the lower rent or mortgage payment: companionship, extended family, fun for both you and the kids, and a wonderful sense of support.

If you're going to date, you might as well try to go out with men who earn a decent income. I'm not a snob, just practical. Remember, it's not just you anymore. There was wisdom in what our mothers told us when they said, "You can fall in love with a rich man just as easily as a poor one." At least give it a shot. And, if his heart isn't as big as his pocketbook—lose him!

There is nothing like making it on your own, though, for feeling really strong and independent. Keep reaching higher. Go back to school if that's a desire and an option. I know it seems impossible sometimes, but where there's a will, there's a way. Money can't buy love, but it sure does make things easier. Good luck.

Some Household Hints

- It's your haven. Make it pretty, safe, and warm. This really is doable. Create a place that feels good to be in, because you're going to be there a lot. Flea markets, garage sales, thrift stores— all groovy places to get cool stuff. Make it a family project.

- Keep it organized: dishes washed; the place neat. I'm telling you, this will do wonders for your "craziness" factor.

- If at all possible, once a month line up an inexpensive maid to do the heavy-duty, grunt work. Then, all you have to do is keep it tidy.

- Have house rules. Post them. Make sure the rugrats/teens stick to them. Update as necessary. Give them chores. No ifs, ands, or buts. If they wanna eat, they've gotta pull their own weight. (Kids under two are excused.)

- Keep "their" space and "your" space separate. You absolutely need a place you can retreat to. Keep it beautiful. No toys or crap inside. Get a lock and a "Do Not Disturb" sign.

- If you work a nine-to-five job, try, if at all possible, to get most of your chores and errands done during the week so that your weekends can truly be your time to relax and have fun with your kids.

You Are Not Going Crazy...

I know that you may feel like it sometimes. Okay, you may feel it most of the time. I do. The irony is that only another single mom can really understand what your life is truly like.

I used to feel resentful, hurt, bewildered. Sometimes, I still do. Day in and day out, no one seems to notice what I'm doing. No one ever says, "Oh, Patrice, if you ever need anything, just let me know." I think I'd pass out if they did.

Times have changed since we women took care of all our offspring together as one family while our men went out and hunted deer for dinner. Now we live in isolated prisons that we decorate with art and electronic entertainment, with phones and computers that are our lifeline to the outside world.

We anesthetize ourselves in many different ways. We are a lonely society living unbalanced lives in uncertain times as we move more and more into the frenzy of surviving.

It's natural for us to feel crazy sometimes. In fact, I believe feeling crazy in this insane world is probably a sure sign of sanity. You are fine! I'm not trying to bum you out: I'm just helping you see how okay you really are.

You are fine!

A Day in My Life

"There is a reason why God intended you to find a mate and then have kids—and not the other way around," I told myself for the 57th time while lying on the kitchen floor after banging my head on the freezer door because I was trying to pick up the frozen corn cobs and fish sticks that went flying after my four-year-old son bellowed his orders for a raspberry popsicle. So, there I was on the linoleum seeing stars and looking at the array of frozen kid TV dinners, mini-pizzas, and veggie hamburger patties and thinking, "Patrice, it's come to this!"

One evening, after just arriving home from work, trying to put away groceries, getting some spaghetti going, pulling off Eli's sneakers that sent sand flying across the room, the phone rang. Some guy named Marvin who saw my video at the dating service that I've since quit (not one decent match in two years). So this guy Marvin, who must have selected me before I quit, asks if I'd like to "pop out" for a cocktail. I almost laugh out loud. "Pop out" what's that? I don't "pop" anywhere anymore, let alone to meet some probable loser who I doubt is even cute. I politely decline. The thought of finding a sitter, giving Eli dinner, bathing and pajama-ing him, cleaning myself up, putting away the groceries, and finally "popping out" seems a sadly futile idea. So, as I lie there pondering just how the hell this life I've created is ever going to change, and if indeed I'll ever meet or actually like a man again, the ice that also fell out of the freezer along with the fish sticks starts to melt and I decide I'd better get up. Eli gets his popsicle and I proceed to pour the sauce on top of noodles.

Welcome to my life.

Having a Rich Fantasy Life

It wasn't supposed to be this way. I had it all figured out. For the longest time I just "knew" that I would find "him."

He was going to be rich, wildly creative, and spiritual as well—the kind of guy who meditated with me in the morning after we made passionate, tantric love on our stained-glass inlaid, platform waterbed. I would then be out writing on the redwood deck of our three-story home, perched on the cliffs overlooking Big Sur, and he'd come out in his freshly showered tanned Adonis body with strawberries and cream for me. Together we'd look out over the Pacific, listening to the waves and our collection of wind chimes, and decide if we wanted to go to Bali or to go diving near the Greek Islands for our summer vacation. He'd profess all over again his deep devotion and we'd caress and decide to discuss potential baby names after dinner: swordfish barbecue with some of our most intimate and fabulously interesting, artsy, entertainment industry friends.

I have a rich fantasy life. Try it, it might help you beat the doldrums.

Thoughts on Child Care

You'll need it. Use it. No guilt. Seek out loving people to care for your child. You can find them and it's worth researching. Ask around. Ask lots of questions. Check it out. Be as involved as possible. Look for scholarship help if you need it.

Make the time they spend with you count. This is most precious to children but they also need outside activities and other kids. Preschools, home day care facilities, camps, after-school programs, etc. provide opportunities for your children where they can be safe and feel affection for other caregivers besides you. They will also learn independence, social skills, and how to obey other people's rules. Then the time with you will be even more special. Besides, where else can they do all that cool art and music stuff with their pals?

I don't know why people have such a negative slant on child care. I think it's a very positive experience. My son has loved it, and, the truth is, most of the kids are much better adjusted than many stay-at-home children.

Teenagers—
If You're Not There Yet, You Will Be

From what I've heard, it's really something to look forward to—NOT! As a single mother, it can be an even harder challenge. Even though I still have a few years to go till I'll be able to offer you any authentic help in the teenage department, I asked around for you and the word I've gotten is that it's definitely no picnic. Here are some sage words of advice from our sister SMOTs (Single Mothers of Teenagers).

- Realize that going from childhood to adulthood is a powerful, confusing transition for all teenagers. Cut them and yourself a little slack.

- But not too much slack. With the prevalence of drugs, alcohol, and crime available to your kids at every turn, don't be a wimpy parent! The decisions you make and limits you set now can make the difference between life and death. I'm not trying to be overly dramatic, I just want to make sure I get your attention on this.

- Be their parent, not their "best friend." Pick your battles; blue hair is better than smoking crack. Treat them with respect, so you can get some respect back.

- Let them know that you really are there for them. Have some empathy. They are experiencing so much emotional roller coastering. If you sense something is really off, get some professional help. Be involved. Though they may put up a front of not wanting you around…too bad. The fact is that this may be precisely the time they need you more than ever.

- Regarding sex: uncomfortable as it may be, you must give them all the information they need. Really talk to them. Then all you can do is cross your fingers and hope for the best.

- The good news is that if you keep the channels of communication open, you'll pass through all these stages with less trauma.

- And, speaking of communication, if you ever want to receive or place a call yourself again, you must get them their own phone line. This is a necessity, and, if they really screw up, yanking phone privileges should whip 'em into shape faster than you can believe!

Self-Esteem

Unfortunately, many single mothers experience a real loss of self-esteem. If this has happened to you, it is vital that you regain it as quickly as possible.

Feel good about the job you're doing. Try getting into a support group or finding a loving therapist. Surround yourself with people who care about you. If you don't have any such people in your life, find some, reach out.

I know I seem to keep repeating the above point over and over, but it's absolutely imperative to care for yourself as well as for your children. Know that you are a precious child of God and are truly loved. Pat yourself on the back for your strength and courage. Be proud. You are worthy. There is no shame in being a single mother. Your kids depend on you.

Go right now to a mirror. Take this book with you. Okay. Are you there? Look deep into your own eyes and know that there is deep honor and nobility in what you are doing. You are a beautiful and special person and I really love each and every one of you. I know it sounds sappy, but, I swear, it's true.

Now, please love yourself.

Legal Matters

Do get a good attorney, but be careful. I have seen lives ruined for many years and children caught as pawns in ugly, expensive, pathetic, legal battles where the attorneys get rich and no one ever really wins.

Try not to have judges and courts rule your life. Take control yourself. If there's any possible way, try to come to an agreement without lawyers. Attempt mediation. I'm all for getting what is due you, but I ask you to decide how much you really want to fight.

Again, unless he is a deadbeat dad or abusive, don't try to have it all your way— it doesn't work. The resentment, game playing, and mind screwing that will go on is a big price to pay. Sit down and really decide what your priorities are. Listen to advice from others, but ultimately make your own choices.

This is the greatest advice that I can give you: Choose happiness.

Dealing with the  Ex

If your children's father is still involved in their life, I have some very definite suggestions that might help.

I know that your situations are very different, but as long as your ex loves them, is not abusive, intoxicated, or drugged, as long as you feel that your children can be safe with him, lighten up and be grateful. Kids do need their dads and benefit from their company. I know he pisses you off. You think he's a slime, a lousy husband, a pain in the ass— blah, blah, blah. That's why he's an "ex." If he were great, let's face it, you'd probably still be together. But he gave you your children and he really is not a totally bad human being. Move on with your life. Stop being at war with him. Life is too short and too stressful. You don't want endless battles. And please don't talk badly about him in front of your children. It simply isn't fair. He is their father.

Sometimes, just accepting who he is will free you up so that you can make positive changes in your own life. When you ease up and stop telling him what a shit he is, or (just humor me here and give it a try) even try giving in once in a while, you can almost be guaranteed that he'll become a much nicer and more workable co-parent. Stop having to be right all the time. Instead, choose happiness for all of you and try to get along with him. Hard as it is (and I know that it is), ask that he be blessed. You share your children together. He hurts too. Find common ground: move to a new level of communication. This can be done, even in the worst of situations. However, if you or your children are in any kind of danger, get legal help.

I have seen miracles happen when ex-spouses stop treating each other horribly. Do it for youself. Do it for the kids. Encourage him to be part of their lives. Try to heal. Life can be good again. Believe it or not, you may even become allies. You and this guy are connected for life and that is a long, long, long time. How do you want that life to be?

Life Isn't Fair!

You will spend some time believing that life isn't fair. We all do. That's okay as long as you move on from there. No matter how relieved you may feel getting out of a bad relationship, or, even if you chose from the start to raise your child alone, sometimes it still feels as though the world is full of two-parent families and you're an outsider looking in. It can be very painful.

Even though the masses are slowly waking up to the fact that the "average" family is rapidly changing, sometimes we still feel as though we're from another planet. There are still not enough children's books, movies, or television shows depicting anything except the Ozzie and Harriet stereotype.

Our workload and the emotional toll of being solely responsible for another human being while fending for ourselves sometimes seem immense, even impossible. It's okay to feel your anger, rage, and sadness, but then you have to dust yourself off, pick yourself up, and start all over again.

It is what it is, Babe.

And remember this too: In our worst of situations, compared to the majority of the world, we still live relatively charmed lives. You could be in a ghetto in Calcutta. See the big picture.

It's all a matter of perspective.

Please keep this in mind: It's very easy to blame every screwed-up aspect of our lives on the fact that we are single moms, but you know what? If you get real honest with yourself and look back, sometimes life was really yucky even before you had kids. Next time you hear yourself saying, "If only I wasn't a single mom," stop!

It's just the nature of things.

Now, if any of you simply have no problems—no loneliness, fears, depressions, terrors, or exhaustion, or if you are never just plain pissed-off at trying to be a single mom in the world today—my hat's off to you.

Self-Pity—
Feeling Like the Victim

Having read the previous page, now we're going to really let loose and get some of this off our minds and chests. Here's how we'll do it. Yell this with me. Here we go!

It sucks, it's exhausting, financially draining, impossible, shitty, lonely, scary, boring, wrong, lousy, not how it was supposed to be, too much for one person. Kids are over-rated—messy, ungrateful, little wretches. Why did I ever get into this? How the hell will I get out? I'm trapped. My life is over. Poor, poor me. Yuck! It's unfair. Terrible! I don't deserve this. I'm being punished. God doesn't care. Damn, damn, damn!

There. Okay. That's it. Time's up. Feeling any better? Now, hopefully, we can move on and see what's really possible with our lives.

A Mother Is a Mother

You are a mother first and foremost, pure and simple. You love your kids and want the best for them, and I bet you would even lay down your life for them if necessary. The only difference between you and most other moms is that you don't have a partner helping you. This is only a technicality.

I know that you're the best mother possible for your kids. They don't get much better than you, lady!

Happy Mother's Day, every day!

How to Find a Husband

(Assuming You Want One)

There is no one subject that seems to have as much conflicting information as this one. Here are some of the contradictory bits and pieces of advice I've been given and have tried over the years.

Men like sweet women.

Men like bitches.

There's no such thing as a soul mate.

Never settle for less than your soul mate.

Make a list of all your ideals in a man.

Don't have any concept of what he should be.

You'll never find him if you're looking.

You'll never find him unless you're looking.

You'll know it's right in the first 5 minutes.

You won't know it's right until you've known him for a long time.

Instant chemistry means trouble.

Instant chemistry means it's a go.

Follow your first instincts, they are accurate.
Never listen to your first instincts, they'll
sabotage you.

Be strong and independent, cool and aloof.
Men like passive women who are kind and
loving, who need them.

Never have sex right away.
Let him know how good you are in bed
right from the get-go.

Try personal ads, singles' dances, video dating.
Never do anything to try to find someone—
when it happens, it happens.

I don't know how anyone's supposed to make
sense out of this, yet somehow, every day,
people are meeting and marrying. You gals
are on your own with this one. Obviously, I
still haven't figured it out. I consider it a great
success to find someone I'd like to have dinner with, let alone share my life with. If any
brilliant ideas come to your mind, please let
me know. In the meantime, I wish you all
good fortune in your endeavors.

Teaching the Important Stuff

No matter how busy you are, please, please, please make the time to teach your children the truly important stuff. Reading, writing, history, and math are only a small part of what they need to learn. Here are some guidelines.

Teach them:

- To be kind, loving people.

- To honor their agreements, have integrity, and be responsible for their actions.

- To value life—their own life, other people's lives, and everything else's.

- To be respectful and tolerant of other people's beliefs, skin colors, body size, disabilities, needs, etc...

- In this day and age, especially when the world can look so bleak to youngsters, let them know there are still many wonderful possibilities, adventures, dreams, and opportunities awaiting them.

- Teach them to have some form of spirituality—connection to the Earth, to the Universe, to God. Without it, nothing has much true value.

- Of course, teach them that love is still the most important thing of all.

  Remember this, too: The best way to teach has always been by example. Maybe it's time we all take our own refresher course?

The Team

You are taking a journey together, your clan and you. They are and will be your little partners in life. Set goals together, fun projects, things to look forward to. They must have duties, chores, and responsibilities, and everyone must chip in to help. Explain the concept that you are a team that wants a successful, happy homelife together. Use their skills and talents. Keep the team spirit.

As a matter of fact, many studies show that children from single-mother homes are often brighter, more independent, respectful, resourceful, and socially adept, and that they mature faster than those in two-parent families. Who knew?!

Yes, You Are a Family

It is imperative to let your children know that what makes a family a family is love, security, and happiness, not how many people live under one roof. Just because your family may look different from many of their friends, it is still their family.

Make sure to befriend other single mothers and their children. Make sure that your children have friends from families like yours. Create rituals and special events that they can cherish always and holidays they will remember.

Do things like other families: go camping, take vacations, and go to gatherings. Get together with your extended groups and spread the love. Get creative. Find books that depict single-mother homes or make up your own stories. Have fun. A family is such a special creation. Enjoy every moment.

Part Two

The
Workbook

Prayer for a Single Mom

Use this whenever you want to. The more you use this prayer, the better your life can be. Please address this prayer to whatever higher source you are comfortable with.

Dear _____,

Please hear my call. I thank you for this gift of motherhood, this gift that many women will never be granted.

Please let me know that you are with me at all times, and especially at those times when I feel lost, angry, scared, exhausted, and lonely.

Please help me remain strong and full of love for my children, who depend on me for the most formative years of their lives.

Please remind me to feel gratitude and joy and to see the humor all around me, for, as you know, this is the hardest job I've ever undertaken. I know you must have a lot of confidence in me to entrust such precious beings in my care.

Please guide me and send me drops of your grace—be it friends, blessings, miracles—to help me in this path of single motherhood. And, most important, let me know (whoever and whatever you are) that you are with us and love us and are proud of us. For to raise and give love to your sentient children is an honor and surely the most important thing I shall do in this lifetime. And, it is my gift and duty back to you.

Amen

Dear _____,

Help!

Amen

Nice Things
You Can Do for a Single Mom

Xerox this list and send it anonymously to
people, or just tell them. Unfortunately, most
folks are clueless. They need suggestions.

- Tell her you admire her and what an amazing
  job she's doing.

- Offer to baby-sit, or to take the kids to school
  once in a while. Any help is needed and will
  be appreciated.

- Ask her how she's doing and then really listen. Hug her, laugh with her, give her a
  shoulder to cry on.

- Invite her and her kids to have dinner with
  you. Invite her and her children for outings,
  fun events, etc. She needs extended family.
  Especially on Sundays and holidays. These are
  her toughest times. Weeknights are pretty
  boring, too.

- Let her know that she can count on you in an
  emergency.

- Occasionally, ask her what she needs. Just the
  asking will help her feel loved and cared
  about.

- If you are a man or have one in your life, share, be a friendly "big brother" or "uncle" to her kids. Even if their father is still involved in their lives, most children of single-mother homes need, want, and love more male energy.

- Talk to her about her children. Notice how special, funny, smart, kind they are. One of the saddest things for a single mom is that there aren't many people to share the pleasures of her children with. Be one of them.

- Be a friend, period!

- Buy her this book if she doesn't already own it.

  Thanks in advance for your help. Spread the word on this one. Perhaps, in time, people will wake up and be more supportive of us. It's worth a try.

Goals and Dreams to Keep You Going

With examples. Update as necessary.

Today, I will:

1. Have an iced mocha and relax for fifteen minutes while reading this book.

2. _____

_____

3. _____

_____

4. _____

_____

5. _____

_____

6. _____

_____

7. _____

_____

This weekend, I will:

1. Plant spring flowers with the kids.

2. _____

_____

3. _____

_____

4. _____

_____

5. _____

_____

6. _____

_____

7. _____

_____

Next month, I will:

1. Get a gorgeous new haircut.

2. _____

   _____

3. _____

   _____

4. _____

   _____

5. _____

   _____

6. _____

   _____

7. _____

   _____

8. _____

   _____

9. _____

   _____

Next year, I will:

1. Take the kids to Hawaii.

2. _____
   _____

3. _____
   _____

4. _____
   _____

5. _____
   _____

6. _____
   _____

7. _____
   _____

8. _____
   _____

9. _____
   _____

In five years, I will:

1. Quit my job and start a painting career.

2. _____
   _____

3. _____
   _____

4. _____
   _____

5. _____
   _____

6. _____
   _____

7. _____
   _____

8. _____
   _____

9. _____
   _____

When the kids are grown, I will:

1. Go around the world.

2. _____

    _____

3. _____

    _____

4. _____

    _____

5. _____

    _____

6. _____

    _____

7. _____

    _____

You know, incredible things can happen when you write down your goals and your dreams. Try it. Let me know what happens.

The Promise

(To be read in times of need)

I, Patrice Karst, author of this book, single
mother of Elijah Karst and sister single
mother to you all, do promise you this:

You _____ will survive and

your name

flourish and have many happy, glorious
times ahead.

In addition, I promise that together we can
draw upon each other's strengths by just
remembering our sisterhood in our
thoughts and prayers.

We will feel an amazing sense of accom-
plishment raising our children and we'll all
have a lot of great laughs and war stories to
share at the end.

The Contract

(Please sign and reread often)

I, _____, do commit
                    your name
myself to taking this life one day at a time.

I promise to remember what an important
job I'm doing and, at the same time, to be
gentle with myself. I further commit myself
to create support around me, to nurture
myself no matter what, to love my children
with all my heart, and to make our home
filled with laughter and joy. In times of dis-
tress, I will pull out this book, reread my
favorite parts, and draw upon the power of
all the single mothers in the world strug-
gling alongside me. Also, I will remember
to pat myself on the back often for doing
my job so well. I will also remember that
the universe has a miraculous plan in mind
for me that is unfolding perfectly.

Signed: _____
                    your signature

Date: _____

Support Phone Numbers

People who love me and care for me whom I can call on for a kind word or in an emergency.

1. _____   _____

2. _____   _____

3. _____   _____

4. _____   _____

5. _____   _____

6. _____   _____

7. _____   _____

8. _____   _____

9. _____   _____

10. _____   _____

Your Inner Sanctuary

Set aside ten minutes, light a candle, put on some relaxing music, light incense, shut the door, and turn off the light. Either lie down or sit down comfortably.

Imagine yourself in any kind of peaceful setting. It could be by a glistening lake or on a balmy beach in the moonlight or in a misty garden at dawn.

Just be there for a while. There is no other place to go, nothing to do, no one around. Feel the air. Hear the sounds of nature. Feel the ground underneath you. Breathe in and out, out and in.

Just hang out here, letting your thoughts pass by in your mind like clouds. Keep letting them float by. Don't hold on. Breathe. See whatever inner guidance or feelings come up for you.

This is your special inner sanctuary that you can go to anytime you desire. Keep breathing, in and out. Thank yourself for this time and open your eyes to the outer world once more.

Come back here often, daily, if possible.

Affirmations

Many people swear by affirmations. Just get out some paper and write these over and over while watching TV or whatever.

I, _____, take life one day at a time and feel great.

I, _____, am an amazing, loving, happy mother.

I, _____, have plenty of time, money, and romance in my life.

I, _____, am creating my dream life.

I, _____, look for-ward to the miracles that lie just around the corner.

Make up your affirmations. No limits.
Go wild if you want to!

_____

_____

_____

_____

_____

_____

_____

_____

_____

_____

_____

_____

_____

_____

Wish List

Consider me your fairy godmother—I deliver.
Come on, go for it! Anything and everything
is acceptable. (And, again, something very
powerful can really happen when you commit to paper your wishes and desires.)

_____

_____

_____

_____

_____

_____

_____

_____

_____

_____

_____

_____

_____

My Gratitude List

There are always things we can be grateful for. List them here and refer to this list whenever you need reminding. (The more you focus on these, the better everything else in your life will look.)

I am grateful for...

_____

_____

_____

_____

_____

_____

_____

_____

_____

_____

_____

_____

Precious & Funny Things My Child Says That I Will Remember Forever

You'll be so glad to have a record of some of these. Just jot down the key words, the rest will all come back to you.

_____

_____

_____

_____

_____

_____

_____

_____

_____

_____

_____

_____

_____

Shit List

This is a safe place to air your gripes and list the perpetrators who cause you any grief. Come on, let it out. You have every right to do this. It's good for you.

_____

_____

_____

_____

_____

_____

_____

_____

_____

_____

_____

_____

_____

_____

My Dreams for My Children and Their World

This will help keep the focus on what we're all doing this for. Think big.

_____

_____

_____

_____

_____

_____

_____

_____

_____

_____

_____

_____

_____

_____

_____

Words of Love to My Kids

Your kids can read this later on in life and
they can hear the love you had for them.

_____

_____

_____

_____

_____

_____

_____

_____

_____

_____

_____

_____

_____

_____

Words of Wisdom
I'd Like to Pass On

Write down some of the things that have helped you in your journey. You might actually help someone else some day.

_____

_____

_____

_____

_____

_____

_____

_____

_____

_____

_____

_____

_____

_____

The Countdown

It might help you to use this chart to realize that by the time your child hits eighteen, you'll be free. Well, legally and technically, anyway. It helps to know that freedom is in sight.

On every birthday, place a checkmark.

❑ Birth to 1	❑ 10
❑ 2	❑ 11
❑ 3	❑ 12
❑ 4	❑ 13
❑ 5	❑ 14
❑ 6	❑ 15
❑ 7	❑ 16
❑ 8	❑ 17
❑ 9	❑ 18

Congratulations!

I knew you could do it.

Go out and celebrate! Drinks are on me!!

You made it!

Who Are You?

You are many people besides just a mother! Sometimes, writing down some of the other aspects of yourself helps to remind you that you have many gifts and talents that you shouldn't forget.

Example:

I, Patrice Karst, am:
- A mother
- A belly dancer
- A sensuous, passionate woman
- An author
- A great friend
- A philosopher
- A spiritual seeker
- An awesome lasagna maker

Now, your turn.

I, _____, am:

_____

_____

_____

_____

_____

_____

_____

_____

_____

_____

_____

_____

_____

_____

_____

_____

Your Cheering Section

I know you probably don't hear any of this stuff often enough, if at all. So, I want you to picture me standing in front of you, exclaiming with loads of passion...

You can do it!

I know how hard you're working.

You're all that and more!

Bravo! Way to go!

Such incredibly lucky kids you have

What an inspiration!

I'm so impressed!

God, you're good!

What a woman!

Part Three

In
Closing

Getting Serious for a Moment

To have the honor of caring for a child, regardless of how the child comes to us, is the most important thing we will ever do. It must be our number one priority for now.

Our children are innocent and in need of our love and guidance in the ways of the world so that they will be safe. They in turn will teach us what love truly means and will provide us with the deepest experience of human intimacy possible.

I wish I could cover every possible thing we will ever need to know. I can't. But together we will learn from one another. Sometimes we will make mistakes. We will slip and fall, and get up over and over again. We will rise to this occasion because somehow we were chosen for this job. Let us be proud of our strength and raise the children well. They are the future.

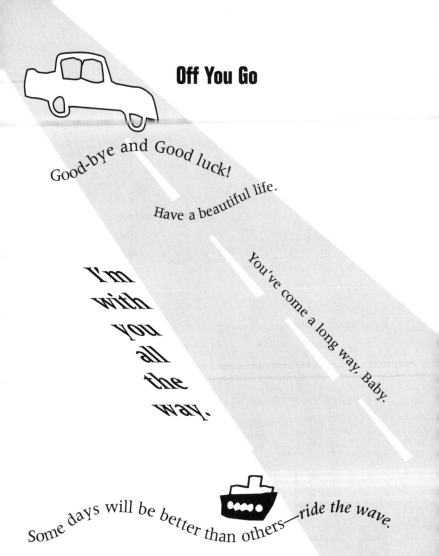

Off You Go

Good-bye and Good luck!

Have a beautiful life.

You've come a long way, Baby.

I'm
with
you
all
the
way.

Some days will be better than others—ride the wave.

May your journey be blessed.

YOU
go
Girl!

You're never given more than you can handle.
You may sometimes feel like this is debatable.

Passing on the Word

If this book has helped you in any way, and God, I hope it has, please tell other single mothers about it, whether they're thinking about becoming a single mother or are one now. We need to look out for each other.

Read them the parts you think will help them, uplift them, whatever. Better yet, buy them the book. It will be a gift they will thank you for.

There's not a whole lot of help out there for us—that's one of the reasons I chose to write this book.

I know this is quite a plug. But, then again, who better to plug it? And, the fact is, it's a book I would have loved to have had during the past eight years. We need to continue to laugh together, cry together, and, most of all, learn to thrive together. Let's go!

My Family

Here is my family.
Much love to yours!

Picture of Elijah and me.

Stay in Touch

I really meant it when I said I'm here for you.
Please write to me. I'd love to get your letters.

You can reach me at:
  Patrice Karst
  P.O. Box 9055
  Calabasas, CA 91372
  singlemothers4u@aol.com

Or:
  The Crossing Press
  P.O. Box 1048
  Freedom, CA 95019

I'm also available for speaking engagements
and would love to do so.

                    So long, for now.
                         Take care.
              It's been my pleasure.

Suggested Reading List

These three books will bring you lots of important information and much joy and encouragement.

Operating Instructions by Anne Lamott, Fawcett-Columbine, 1993.

In Praise of Single Parents by Shoshana Alexander, Houghton Mifflin, 1994.

The Complete Single Mother by Andrea Engber and Leah Klungness, Ph.D., Adams Publishing, 1995.

BOOKS BY THE CROSSING PRESS

It's Not Fair!

By Dominique Jolin

It's not fair! a little girl complains to her father, who listens patiently and in the end points out the one thing she has that no one else has-him! Sure to make both children and parents smile.

$12.95 • Hardcover • Ages 4-8 • full-color illus. • ISBN 0-89594-780-3

Morningtown Ride

Words and Music by Malvina Reynolds; Illus. by Michael Leeman

The train to Morningtown takes sleepy children safely through the night in Malvina Reynolds' classic lullaby, enhanced with beautiful illustrations.

$14.95 • Hardcover • ISBN 0-89594-763-3

Walk When the Moon is Full

By Frances Hamerstrom; Illustrations by Robert Katona

An unusual offering for parents in search of ways to share nature with their children. Careful black-and-white drawings match the hushed mood of the moonlit walks.—Booklist

$6.95 • Paper • ISBN 0-912278-84-6

To receive a current catalog from The Crossing Press please call toll-free, 800-777-1048.
Visit our Web site: **www.crossingpress.com**